Beyond the Mirror

Other works by this author:

From the Heart: Reflections on Life

**From the Heart:
Reflections on Life**

by Diana Spektor

For more information, please visit
www.lulu.com/spotlight/DianaSpektor

Beyond the Mirror

Diana Spektor

2015

First Printing: 2015

ISBN 978-1-312-69812-3

Photo of the mirror by: Marcin Sylwia Ciesielski

Diana Spektor, Publisher

Toronto, Ontario

www.facebook.com/diana.spektor.writer

She left the web, she left the loom,
She made three paces through the
room,
She saw the water-lily bloom,
She saw the helmet and the plume,
She look'd down to Camelot.
Out flew the web and floated wide;
The mirror crack'd from side to
side;
"The curse is come upon me," cried
The Lady of Shalott.

— Alfred, Lord Tennyson, *The Lady
of Shalott*

Contents

Acknowledgements

No one can give you confidence: they can only build up the confidence you already have. Yet a strong support system in all aspects of life – personal, professional, and everything in-between – can mean the difference between success and failure, especially for a fledgling writer such as myself.

So, I would first like to express my appreciation to The Group of Five. In no particular order, to Kat Polzun for steering me towards writing and editing and being there every step of the way; to Liuba Krichevsky for the fun yet meaningful exchange of life stories in essay form; to Yuri Spektor for the beautiful book covers and spending hours on the overall production process; to Colan Nielsen for the literary discussions and believing in both my professional and creative writing; and to Luba Bryushkova for the constructive criticism that helps me be sure of my choices. In fact, the simple question of "How is your writing going?" may not seem like much, but to me it means a lot.

I would also like to thank the head of my [somewhat imaginary] marketing department, Jamila Spektor. Without your tireless efforts, my book sales would be significantly lower. Your unconventional sales strategy with the slogan "My daughter is talented – please read her books" shows great dedication that I could never forget.

Finally, I would like to thank all my other current and future readers. A writer always needs a relatively unbiased audience. After all, all the world's a stage, is it not?

Prologue

The woman stood in her living room, looking around it with regret. She knew that she will not be coming back. With a sigh, she turned her back on the room one last time and began walking up the stairs at a brisk pace. Briefly stopping at the door to her bedroom to pick up her suitcase, she continued her ascent to the attic.

There it was: The Mirror. To her, it was never just an object with which to see one's own reflection. It was so much more than that.

Once again stopping at the piano in her attic – a strange place to keep it, the average observer might say – she took a letter out of her pocket and placed it on the keys where she was sure that the intended recipient would find it. Then, she stepped over the threshold and was never seen again...

Imperfect

Why am I doing this? I thought for the hundredth time that day alone, as I sat researching maps of London, England. My home office, also known as the corner of my living room near the window, was getting dark. I was working late again, yet considering that my life was going nowhere, I preferred not to allow my mind to be unoccupied for too long.

My official job title is School Bus Route Planner. Every week, my boss sends me bus routes and a list of addresses of new students, and I must incorporate them into the existing routes and devise the quickest path between them. The most frustrating part is that there are frequent instances where I've just completed a new bus route, and suddenly I'm notified that a student has moved to a new address so I have no choice but to start the route-making process all over again. Even on a good day, the job is tedious and the hours are long, but I can work from home, which is what I originally liked about the job description. It also requires no post-secondary education, and considering that I hold an unwanted Bachelor's Degree in biology, this was good news for me.

Ever since I could remember, I've wanted to become a classical concert pianist one day. I studied musical theory and took piano lessons since I was five years old, and my dream was to attend The Royal Conservatory of Music here in London or perhaps even The Julliard School in New York City. My parents, however, had other plans. According to them, music is impractical and I should instead aspire to the family tradition of being a dentist. I am a dental heiress – soon to become a mental heiress – destined to spend my life touching other people's teeth, among other things. The entire enterprise made me feel sick to my stomach, not to mention the fact that I never quite mastered math and science back in school and only obtained my degree due to my father's insistent tutoring. After graduation, I obediently walked into my parents' dental office to begin my training. I listened to a description of the common dental problems, watched my mother's thorough examination of a particularly bad-tempered old lady with dentures, and I walked right back out. To this day, more than three years later, I don't think that my parents have fully forgiven me.

I closed my laptop in exasperation, somewhat louder than I had intended. I stood up from my chair and walked over to the window, only to catch a glimpse of the last rays of the afternoon sun filtering through the clouds. I began absent-mindedly pulling at one of the ribbons with which I tie back my curtains, still watching the beautiful spring day nearing its end. The maple trees in the park across the street were starting to grow new leaves, the cherry blossoms were almost in full bloom, and many people were still out on their early evening strolls. The outside was an image of perfection. The inside of my little apartment was chaos, as I once again thought back to what happened only eight short days ago...

It was just past dawn and I was peace-fully sleeping when I was suddenly awoken by the sound of something repeatedly scraping across my window. My first thought was that someone was breaking into my home, and I jumped off my bed in fear. Then I saw small rocks flying up-wards, still hitting the glass, and I smiled as I walked across my room, opened the window and looked down.

"Took you long enough! Good morn-ing, Sleeping Beauty!" shouted my friend of sixteen years who has also been my boy-friend for nine of those years. Since the day I met him, he has always had the annoying habit of looking shamelessly happy both in and out of context. This morning seemed to be in the out-of-context category.

"Oliver! Do you realize what time it is?" I yelled back.

He looked at his watch. "It's very early, that's true. In that case, why are you yelling? You could wake your neighbours!"

He looked back up at me with a falsely condescending smirk.

He's hopeless, I thought to myself as I gave him an evil glare and closed the window. I then quickly changed, made myself look as human as I possibly could at this ungodly hour of 5:45 a.m., then I locked the door to my apartment and walked downstairs.

There he was, my wonderful, kind Oliver, obediently waiting for me in the lobby. I've known him my entire life and loved him for his personality, yet I've never stopped being mesmerized by his appearance – especially his eyes, which were even more green than usual every time he wore something green, like today. Without saying a word, I walked into his embrace and felt more at home than I ever had anywhere else.

I quickly recovered my wits, however, and stepped away, saying, "Seriously, there are these things called a phone and an intercom. Maybe you've heard of them?"

"Yes, I might have," he said with a smile. Then his face became serious and he continued, "I do apologize for waking you, but we have to go!"

"Where?"

"Just trust me – I have something to show you!"

"You know I hate surprises," I replied. "Or at least save them for daylight hours next time."

He laughed. "There's no next time. Please, Silvana, I went through a lot to do this for you."

"Using guilt to manipulate me – well played," I replied, poking his arm. "Fine, just let me go get my jacket," I said, and ran back up to my second-floor apartment.

I had to admit that I was excited. Oliver was very talented at planning the most ridiculous things, which usually ended up being memorable. So, when he took me to the zoo and proceeded to ask one of the workers to let us in to see the new white tiger cub, I was only curious. It has been quite some time since I stopped being concerned for his sanity. Also, considering that he was the head veterinarian at a tiger sanctuary, I've been introduced to many animals over the years that we have been together. Yet I certainly did not expect the whirlwind of events that were about to happen.

The zoo employee – named John, according to his name tag – led us through the service building and into a room referred to as the nursery. In one of the cages was the most beautiful tiger cub I've ever seen. John unlocked the cage and, with a nod at Oliver's word of thanks, left us alone. Oliver picked up the tiger cub and offered it to me, speaking in an unusually formal manner: "Silvana, allow me to introduce this little girl. She is only three months old, but she is already as smart, beautiful, and strong-willed as you are. So, we decided to name her Silvana, and I hope that you two will become great friends."

I took the tiger cub out of his arms, touched by the incredibly thoughtful gesture. "That's really sweet. Thank you so much!" I replied, scratching the tiger behind the ear. She purred like the cat that she was, and I took it as agreement with my statement.

I had just opened my mouth to ask for more information when Oliver continued:

"Wait, there's more. See if there's anything unusual about her collar."

I took a closer look and saw a beautiful ring attached to the tiger's collar. I looked back at Oliver to express my confusion and found him kneeling in front of me. Seeing that he had my attention, he said, "I know this is sudden, but you are the best thing that ever happened to me and I can't imagine my life without you. Silvana Doyle, will you marry me?"

I was momentarily stunned into silence. Then I carefully placed the tiger back into his arms and said, "I'm sorry. I can't."

I turned away and ran out of the room, but not before I could register the pain and confusion on his face.

Luckily, I lived only ten minutes away from the zoo. By the time I heard him chase after me and start calling my name, I was nearly home. I ran into my apartment, promptly slamming and locking the door, and collapsed in tears onto a chair in my living room. Oliver followed me and sat outside my door that entire day, until I threatened to call the police. I walked over to the window to watch his departure, and it nearly killed me to see him walking away with no backward glance. Yet I knew that what I did simply had to be done. There was no way to make him understand that he was too perfect and I was not nearly perfect enough.

Intuition

My thoughts were interrupted by the ringing of my phone, which I haven't been answering throughout my emotional turmoil all week. The only thing that kept me from drowning in the waves of despair was my dog Arch. The miniature poodle's full name is Archibald, a result of my brief interest in Gothic literature three years ago when Oliver gave him to me as a graduation present. The dog was a somewhat painful reminder of what I had lost, and yet I loved Arch regardless of his origins.

After the last notes of Clair de Lune died down and the room fell silent once again, I walked over to my desk to see whether whoever called also left a message. Sure enough, I heard the dreaded voicemail message from Mr. Feng: "Sylvia! I'm sending you a list of student addresses for that new school that opened near Trafalgar Square. I want three new bus routes done by Friday. Goodbye."

All I could do in response was sigh in annoyance, and as my phone began listing options on what to do with the message, I pressed the number 7 to delete it.

I only met Mr. Feng once, during my

interview, and he made a lasting impression on me – one that I would not wish upon my worst enemy. His black eyes immediately reminded me of a spider cornering its prey, and his hand, during the mandatory handshake, was unnaturally cold. Had I still been in high school that day, I could have sworn that he was a vampire. Even his name made no sense. "Feng" implies an East-Asian origin, yet his appearance was ethnically vague. His age was also quite vague, although I would guess him to be in his fifties. He was not a tall man, but his very presence seemed to emanate power and potential evil. His voicemail messages have always been rude and demanding, and he refuses to learn my name. After two years, he still calls me Sylvia.

I sat back down at my desk, still in the darkness of early dusk, and opened my laptop once again. As I logged into my email inbox to see the assignment from Mr. Feng, I noticed a new email message from my best friend Skylar. I'm ashamed to admit that I've been ignoring her all week, and while she tried to let me have the space I needed, I knew that my lengthy silence was worrying her. In the message, she asked me to at least tell her that I haven't harmed myself in any way. This made me smile: Skylar always jumped to conclusions, but I knew that her heart was definitely in the right place.

I met her in fourth-grade music class. I had just moved to London and my parents enrolled me in a prestigious private school. I was the first to walk into the music classroom, and when I saw the beautiful piano standing in the center of the room I simply had to play it. As I sat down on the piano bench and played the first few notes in a song of my own composition, however, I heard laughter and was shocked to discover that the room had begun to fill with my new classmates. I quickly stood up and lowered my head in shame, but then I felt someone touch my shoulder and a voice said, "Don't listen to them. I think you are very talented. Want to be friends?"

I looked up to see a girl with light-brown hair, hazel eyes and, most importantly, a friendly smile. Ever since that fateful day, she was like a sister to me, and you can't push someone like that away no matter how much you desire solitude. So, instead of replying to Skylar's email I decided to call her.

She responded very quickly: "Silvana, hi! Are you okay?"

I laughed. "Yeah, I'm fine. I'm sorry I haven't been responding to your calls and text messages. I just read your email and decided to call you back," I explained. "How are you?"

"I'm great, now that I finally heard from you. How are you dealing with-- you know."

"Honestly, I'm trying not to think about it so I can get some work done. Not only does he still call me ten times a day, so does his mother. I really want to talk to them, but I just can't."

"It's okay, we don't have to talk about it," Skylar said, knowing my emotional limits and not pushing me beyond what I can handle.

"Thanks." I paused. "Do you remember my Aunt Margaret?"

Long experience preventing her from being baffled by my sudden change of subject, Skylar laughed. "Do I! With all due respect, the woman was terrifying. I always thought she needed more bran in her diet, but that's just me."

This time I laughed so hard that I almost dropped my phone. When I had sufficiently calmed down, I said, "Thank you, I really needed that. Anyways, you know that my parents have been trying to sell her house after she passed away, right? For some reason, potential buyers always find something wrong with the place."

"That's unfortunate. That old house is beautiful. Why are you suddenly bringing it up?

"I was thinking of going there to look through her old things. She was a collector of various antiques, and my parents wanted me to see if there's anything I'd like to keep before they try selling it."

"That sounds exciting! Do you want me to help you?"

"I was hoping you would. She had an old mirror that I really liked when I was a child, and if it's still there and in good condition, I'd like to take it. Would Saturday afternoon work for you?"

"Yes, that sounds good. I'll meet you there," Skylar replied.

"Great! Thanks. See you then," I concluded the conversation and hung up the phone.

The Letter

The next few days were uneventful. I finished the bus routes and sent them to Mr. Feng. Aside from my brief walks with Arch three times a day, I haven't had the energy to go anywhere. Although, after surviving on tuna and bananas for over a week, I finally went to the grocery to get myself some real food.

I was relieved that Oliver and his mother had stopped calling me, and I was happy that they could not meet with my parents to dissect the whole situation and try to solve it. My parents were currently in Sweden at a lengthy dental conference, and aside from verifying my well-being twice a week, they haven't spoken to me much.

On Saturday morning, I woke up earlier than usual to prepare for the busy day ahead of me. Skylar had called me to say that she couldn't join me because she had a severe headache, and although she apologized and tried to reschedule, I decided to go alone. I learned long ago to obey my intuition, and today it was telling me not to delay my trip. So, I dressed in my old jeans and a comfortable sweater, packed lunches for myself and Arch, and drove to Aunt Margaret's house on the other side of the city. All I knew about her is that she was my father's sister who, I now suspected, was slightly bipolar. Her preferred method of communication was criticism in a raised voice, yet sometimes she could be surprisingly kind and loving. These mood swings were what scared me when I was a child, and I was happy that I hadn't seen her since I was twelve. When she was killed in a train accident last year, I did not grieve for long and, surprisingly, neither did my parents.

I stopped the car in front of my aunt's house. Upon closer examination, it proved to be extremely dilapidated, as if it hadn't been used in decades as opposed to thirteen months. From the street, however, it looked like a regular Victorian home, exactly like all the ones surrounding it. Dark clouds have invaded the previously sunny sky and it looked like it would start raining at any moment, so I hurriedly took my bag and Arch from the back seat and ran to the porch. After unlocking the door with the key I took from my parents' house on the way, I walked inside only to stop in my tracks when I heard someone playing the piano in this house that was supposed to have been empty.

My first instinct was sensible: to walk out as quietly as possible and perhaps call the police. Just as I was about to do so, my dog suddenly took off like a rocket and began running up the stairs, barking madly.

"Arch! Come back here!" I yelled in surprise and ran after him, only briefly pausing to close the front door. Even as I followed my dog up to the attic, I began to wonder about this intruder. Arch hadn't sensed anything out of the ordinary until a few seconds after we came in. *Also, why would someone break into a house just to play the piano?* I thought to myself.

There was no sign of Arch as I approached the final set of stairs leading to the attic. The door closing off these stairs, usually closed, was left ajar. I haven't heard any other human sounds and the piano had stopped playing, yet I walked up the stairs cautiously and peered through the attic doorway. The room was empty except for a white grand piano, a mirror, and my dog. There was nothing else in the room where a person could hide, so I relaxed slightly as I walked inside.

"Arch, what's wrong? Are you okay?" I asked him.

He wagged his tail in response and began playing with his own reflection in the mirror. Normally I would have played with him, but I was entranced by the room I hadn't seen in over thirteen years. For as long as I could remember, Aunt Margaret had a piano even though she couldn't play it. This was almost as mysterious as the mirror in her attic, which was taller than me even now and encased in a beautiful golden frame with various mythological creatures drawn along it – centaurs, mermaids, unicorns, to name a few. When I was a little girl, I always thought that this mirror was magical.

Finally drawing my gaze away from the mirror, I looked around the room once again and noticed something I hadn't seen earlier – an envelope lying on top of the piano keys. I walked closer and picked it up and, seeing that it was addressed to me, carefully tore the envelope and unfolded two sheets of paper with neat writing on both sides of each. The letter said:

My dear Silvana,

Your father will be very angry with me for sending you this letter, but you are not a child anymore and there are some things about our family that you must learn before it's too late.

Do you remember the mirror in my attic? You found it when you were only three years old, during one of your family vacations. Back then, I was still allowed to spend time with you, and I did not have to hide who I truly am. You were always an obedient child, but one afternoon your parents left you with me while they went to take care of a few errands and you would not listen to a word I said. I soon had no choice but to lock you in the attic until you promised to behave yourself. I'm not proud of my methods, but that was the day you discovered the mirror and instantly fell in love with it. At first you would play your childish games there during your visits, pretending to be a magical princess, and when your family moved back to London, I had my piano moved into the attic so that you could practice here whenever you wanted. The mirror always seemed to inspire you. Then one day when you were twelve, your mother came to pick you up and you told her that a lady inside the mirror spoke to you, and that was the last time your parents allowed you to see me...

This part of the story suddenly reminded me of how my fear of Aunt Margaret's mood swings never stopped me from wanting to be in her house. When I was suddenly forbidden to see her, I pleaded with my parents to at least borrow the mirror that so mesmerized me, but their decision was final and they would not yield.

One day when I was about fifteen, I overheard my father yelling at someone on the phone in his home office: "No! My daughter is human and we intend to keep her that way. ... Did you not hear me? I said... No, she will not be trained only to put herself in danger. I won't allow it! Goodbye!"

Fuming, he hung up the phone. I had never seen my father this angry before, and I was glad that he hadn't noticed my accidental eavesdropping.

Remembering the incident now, I was more confused than ever, so I decided to finish reading the letter.

... You see, my dear girl, our family is descended from a long line of the protectors of a place called Kaleidos. In fact, the royal family of Kaleidos is growing smaller, and that is why I wanted you to train and develop your magical powers. Your father was King and High Protector of our land until certain circumstances made him renounce his powers and move into the mortal world forever. I followed your family here because I thought you would need additional protection from someone who wishes you harm. If

you had your magic even in the mortal world, you would at least be able to defend yourself should the need ever arise. Unfortunately, you will lose your powers at the stroke of midnight on your 26th birthday, which leaves me no time to tell you this story in person and teach you everything you need to know. I sincerely hope that you will one day find your way back to our world and take up your rightful place as Queen and High Protector of Kaleidos before it's too late. For now, I will have to go back there myself to see what I can do.

Eternally yours,
Aunt Margaret.

P.S. I apologize for the trouble you have surely been having with your hair. The spell I placed on it was only meant to make it easier to hide you in plain sight. I wanted to keep you safe from HIM!

The letter was dated December 29 – the day my aunt supposedly died in a train crash on her way home from Ireland. The story, while seemingly linear and well-organized, had several plot holes. Then there were Aunt Margaret's claims to be speaking of real events. The sensible part of my mind made me wonder how serious her mental condition had been to make her hallucinate to this extent. My traitorous intuition, however, was leading my mind in a different direction, eventually forcing me to wonder, *Could she be telling the truth?*

Beyond the Mirror

Confused, I folded up the letter and decided to play the piano. It always helped clear my head. Yet just as I sat down on the piano bench and touched the keys, the mirror began to shimmer and a voice of an indiscernible gender began speaking in a language I could not identify. I immediately remembered the lady who supposedly spoke to me through the mirror according to my aunt's letter, and I began to question my own sanity. I even pinched my arm to make sure I was awake.

My dog, who calmly sat beside the mirror this entire time, began barking madly once more. Before I could stop him he ran straight through the mirror and I had no choice but to follow him, too shocked to ponder how this could even be possible. I stepped over the bottom section of the frame – which, I later realized, served as a threshold into the other world – and fell into approximately three feet of snow. The next thing I knew is that I was being hauled to my feet none too gently and an unpleasantly familiar voice said, "Well, it's about time you arrived, Miss Doyle."

I looked up into the eyes of the man I least wanted or expected to see, especially in this alternate universe I was not entirely sure I hadn't imagined.

"Mr. Feng?" I asked, shocked.

He was dressed in clothing that could only be described as medieval, including the traditional metal armour, complete with a helmet and sword belt. In the middle of his chest was a large letter C entwined with a black snake. I was distracted from what was obviously a crest of some sort, however, by the sword he held in his hand.

"'Mr. Feng' was my alias in the mortal world. Here, I am known as King Julian Cromwell," said someone who I thought was the owner of a private company providing school buses to the city of London.

I did not know what to say, still processing everything that happened to me in the last hour, and yet he clearly expected a response. "I don't understand. What's going on here? What is this place?" I asked.

"Why don't we escort you to Cromwell Castle to discuss this further? You must be cold, standing here in the snow," said the king with warmth that did not reach his black eyes.

"We?"

It was only then that I noticed the large group of men standing behind Cromwell. Their light silver armour disguised them exceptionally well among the snow-covered spruces, as did their helmets with the visors shut over their faces. They stood as still as statues, and only upon a wave of Cromwell's hand did they begin preparing for departure. Seemingly out of nowhere, all but Cromwell and another man brought forth a white horse and promptly mounted it.

I knew that I had no choice but to go with them, yet being calm and collected in a crisis was not new to me. In a steady voice that did not betray my anxiety, I said to the king, "I will go with you, but first, I would appreciate it if you would lower your sword."

"My apologies, Miss Doyle," he replied. "We wouldn't want to be known for our lack of hospitality."

With that, he turned around and walked to his horse. Meanwhile, I was approached by another man whose face remained covered with the visor of his helmet. He sank into a low bow and spoke: "Would you like your own horse, Miss Doyle, or would you prefer to ride with one of us?"

I hesitated. I had taken riding lessons when I was younger, and hence the transportation did not bother me at all. However, I was anxious about the situation I found myself in, and I was not particularly comfortable with a group of strange men in the middle of a forest.

Sensing the problem, the man detached the sword hanging at his belt and offered it to me. "Would this make you feel safer?" he asked. "You should know that a king's son would never choose to be unarmed if his intentions were not noble."

"Thank you, that's very kind of you," I said, taking the sword. Although I knew close to nothing about sword-fighting, I was confident that I could defend myself if necessary. I also asked for my own horse, silently wondering why they had brought a spare after seeing the prince mount yet another horse.

I attached the prince's sword to one of the leather straps on the saddle, and then placed Arch in the saddle bag. He had stopped barking after we passed through the mirror and remained strangely calm throughout the entire course of the latest events, and only now did he begin to protest by quietly growling at me. I stroked his head and kissed his nose to reassure him, putting on a calm façade for my dog's benefit as well as my own. Yet as I closed the bag, I said in a low voice, "Toto, I have a feeling we are not in Kansas anymore."

Once I had climbed into the saddle, we set off into the forest. I looked back at the clearing and saw for the first time that the portal had disappeared along with Aunt Margaret's mirror.

Cromwell Castle

The king's silent army followed a circuitous path through the ever-darkening trees, and I realized that it was getting close to nightfall. I hoped that these woods had no wolves in them – or worse. This was a magical place, after all. Arch seemed calm enough, as did my horse who obeyed me like no other horse ever had. If the animals did not sense any danger, then I could allow myself to relax and look around. The king rode in the lead, followed by his son, while I was surrounded on all sides by the silent army. I had not asked the prince his name and he did not offer it during our brief conversation, which I thought was strange. I added this to the long mental list of questions I already had about this place.

My wristwatch, which somehow still worked, indicated that we had been riding for almost two hours when we finally reached a clearing in the trees. That was when Cromwell stopped his horse and signaled for his men to stop as well. After a brief conference with his father, the younger Cromwell turned his own horse and rode back towards me. I was able to distinguish the different between them because Cromwell's visor was still raised, while his son's remained shut. As soon as the prince was level with me, our silent procession once again began moving. We cleared the line of trees and began walking through a field, and I was mesmerized by the beauty of my surroundings. Although it was now fully dark, the cloudless sky held a full moon that illuminated the snow-capped mountains on the horizon and, across the snowy field, a medieval castle straight out of a history textbook.

I was so distracted by the scenery that I completely forgot about my companion until he spoke: "Miss Doyle, are you still afraid?"

"I never was," I replied. "I am simply confused. I've just walked through a mirror only to be greeted by a king and his army and brought on a strange journey to a royal palace."

"Does your world not look like this?" he asked, sounding mildly curious.

"It used to look like this a few centuries ago, but today it is very different."

"How so?"

"It's difficult to describe..." I paused. "Can't you ask your father? He apparently spent quite some time in my world."

"That is something you should discuss with him," the prince said, closing himself off from me again.

"No, please talk to me. In fact, you still have not introduced yourself or even shown your face. Is there any reason for this?"

He seemed taken aback by my bluntness but his reply was nothing but courteous: "Please forgive me. My name is Gideon Cromwell and I am heir to the throne of Kaleidos."

Letting go of the reigns, he lifted his visor and turned his head towards me. I was met with a black gaze as chilling as that of his father, and I quickly turned away in horror.

"It's nice to meet you," I said, keeping my own gaze focused on the road ahead.

He did not comment, but I could feel him looking at me for several seconds until I heard him sigh and lower his visor. We rode the rest of the way in silence.

We arrived at the castle after another hour or so. Because it was dark, I was completely taken aback by the sheer size and beauty of the building. It was built from a stone I could not identify in any way aside from the light golden colour, and the tallest towers rose hundreds of feet into the air. The evenly tiled roofs were of a somewhat darker colour, and each tower featured a white flag with the black snake entwined with the letter C, which I now knew stood for "Cromwell." I was still feeling slightly overwhelmed by the day's events, yet I could not help but wonder what the castle had looked like when it was ruled by my father. I was certain that Aunt Margaret's story – if it was actually as real as it currently seemed to be – left out many important details, and I intended to find out what they were. I was so absorbed in my own thoughts that I didn't notice Cromwell and his silent army come to a stop inside the castle's outer walls until I heard a new voice addressing me: "May I help you dismount, my lady?"

I looked down and saw a boy of about fourteen years of age, holding my horse's reigns with his left hand and offering his right hand to me. Although he was clearly a stable boy, his clothing and overall appearance was surprisingly immaculate. That was when I noticed that he did not wear a coat of any kind and was further surprised to find no snow in the castle grounds. I filed this observation with my ever-growing list of questions and replied with a smile, "Thank you, but I can manage it myself."

As I threw one leg over the saddle and easily slid to the ground, I saw that my silent companions had already dismounted and their horses were being led away. By the time I took my dog out of the saddle bag, I noticed that the prince had approached me.

"Miss Doyle, welcome to Cromwell Castle," he declared. "My father will meet you in the Council Chamber with his royal advisor after breakfast tomorrow morning. He --"

"Tomorrow morning? You expect me to stay here overnight?" I interrupted him, losing control over my calm façade at last.

I was going to say more, but I heard a collective gasp from a crowd that seems to have replaced the king and most of his guards within the last two minutes. *How does everyone here move so swiftly and quietly?* I thought to myself.

"How dare you interrupt the prince when he is speaking!" said one of the remaining guards with outrage, lowering his spear and pointing it straight at me.

"Please lower your weapon. Is this how you treat a guest, especially a woman?" I demanded.

"You are no guest! Your family almost destroyed this kingdom until King Cromwell stepped in and saved us all. Be gone!"

shouted a middle-aged woman standing among the new arrivals.

My confusion must have been clearly written on my face, for that was the moment Prince Gideon decided to intervene. He raised his hand, which brought immediate silence, and said, "My beloved subjects, while I appreciate your loyalty to my father, the lady is correct – we do not speak to guests with such disrespect. My sincerest apologies, Miss Doyle."

I nodded in acceptance, and he continued, "Carolyn, please escort our guest to the room in the West tower and have Esmeralda take care of her. Miss Doyle will be needing a late dinner after the long journey. The rest of you, go back to your evening duties."

Before he walked away, the prince bowed to me once more and said, "Good night, Miss Doyle. I promise that tomorrow we will explain everything."

"Good night, Your Highness. And thank you!" I replied with an awkward curtsey.

As the rest of the crowd – all of whom appeared to be servants – quickly dispersed, I was left alone with the woman who had yelled at me earlier. She walked towards me and said, "Let us make one thing clear: While I am the Head of the

Household, I do not serve unwelcome guests. I will provide you with an adequate meal and Esmeralda, your new maid, but I want no more demands from you. And make sure this dog of yours does not make a mess."

Arch growled in response, but I said, "I understand. Thank you."

Satisfied, Carolyn quickly began walking towards one of the side doors. As I started to follow her, I whispered to Arch, "I know. I don't like her either."

Mysterious

The walk across the dark courtyard was short, and before I knew it we were inside the palace kitchens. I was sure that guests were not normally shown this part of the castle but I did not dare mention that to Carolyn, mostly because I was hungry and needed her to feed me. Sadly, the sandwich I had packed this morning was in my bag, which was likely still on Aunt Margaret's piano bench. The women washing and putting away various dishes looked at me with evident curiosity, but no one spoke to either Carolyn or myself, and I assumed that they were as afraid of her as I was.

We exited the kitchens and began ascending a long and winding staircase, and I realized that we were walking straight up into the West tower where my room was supposed to be. Carolyn walked ahead of me at a steady pace without uttering a word, and I did dare betray the fact that I was beginning to feel tired. Yet I also did not dare let Arch walk on his own, fearing Carolyn's anger if he were to make any noise, so I carried my dog the entire way. When we finally reached a doorway at the top of the staircase, Carolyn walked through and immediately stopped at another door in the dark hallway. I did not have the time to look around – all I managed to see was a shiny floor reflecting the candles in sconces hanging at intervals along both walls, disappearing in the darkness ahead – before Carolyn suddenly grabbed my arm and pushed me into the room that I assumed was to be mine throughout the duration of my visit.

"Stay here, *Miss* Doyle," she said with undisguised hostility. "Esmeralda will be here soon with your dinner. Good night."

With that, she walked out, slamming the door behind her.

"Thank you!" I called after her, remaining polite despite my feelings towards the housekeeper.

Finally placing Arch on the floor, I turned around and was immediately amazed by the beauty of the room. It seemed to be a sitting room, with two small couches and a table set between them. The light-green walls were lined with various cupboards, and at one end was a large window overlooking the mountains I had seen on the way here. Across from the window was another door, and as I walked through it I found myself in a room with a large four-poster bed surrounded by light-green curtains. One wall was almost entirely taken up by a huge window with the same view of the beautiful mountains, while another wall held a giant wardrobe that a girl could only dream of. The final wall held a room that could only be the bathroom, and one look inside confirmed my assumption.

My explorations were interrupted by a knock at my front door, and when I opened it I found myself looking at someone who was likely one of the maids. She wore a brown dress with a white apron, and her black hair was held back from her face with a white cap tied with a ribbon. In her hands she held a covered tray with what I assumed was my dinner.

When she saw me, she immediately curtsied and said, "Good evening, Miss Doyle. My name is Esmeralda."

Smiling and stepping aside, I said, "Hello Esmeralda. Come on in. And please, call me Silvana."

"Oh, I couldn't do that!" she replied, walking through the door and turning to face me once again. "Please make yourself comfortable. I've been instructed to tell you that you may wear anything you wish from the wardrobe. I shall set out your dinner, and later I will come back to pick up the tray. Please let me know if you need anything else."

"That's very kind of you. Thank you!" I said, happy to have finally met a genuinely nice person in this strange place.

By the time I changed into a long-sleeved nightgown and walked out from behind the screen meant for that purpose, Esmeralda was standing in my bedroom and examining the jacket and boots I had taken off when I came in. When she saw me, she hastily backed away from the open wardrobe, saying, "I'm sorry, Miss Doyle. I was simply admiring your clothing. A green jacket and brown boots would have camouflaged you quite well in the woods if it weren't for this eternal winter."

"Eternal winter?" I asked.

"It just seems eternal, that's all. Winter always ends very late in Kaleidos," she explained with strange haste. Even more surprising was the panic in her eyes.

Then something clicked. "Wait... Is that why there's no snow within the castle walls? Kaleidos is under a spell?"

Instead of answering my questions, Esmeralda stammered, "I--I'm sorry, pl--please forget I s--said anything. Good night!"

She turned and ran out of the room, leaving me more confused than ever. Of one thing I was sure, however: Something here was very, very wrong.

Knowing that I wouldn't find any more answers tonight, I quickly ate the cheese omelet I found on the dinner tray and gave the plate of sausages to Arch. Then, I began looking through the various cupboards for something that could be used as a bed for him. After a few minutes, I found not only a basket and an extra blanket, but also teacups, an electric kettle, and even a small refrigerator. Clearly, Cromwell brought several modern comforts into his medieval castle, which also included the facilities. Although I had much bigger problems as Carolyn was leading me into the castle, part of my mind was dreading washing my face and hands with recycled water from an old-fashioned wash basin.

As I continued exploring the contents of the cupboards, I must have touched a secret button of some sort because the cupboards on one of the walls slid aside to reveal another room. Although the room was small, three of its walls were entirely covered in bookshelves, and in the middle stood a beautiful grand piano. I walked inside and looked around in awe, for I loved books almost as much as I loved playing the piano. Yet before I could investigate this secret room any further, I noticed the inconspicuous plague above the piano keys: "Property of Annabelle Cromwell."

Annabelle? Could it be referring to my mother? I thought to myself, knowing that at this point nothing would surprise me about this place.

Complications

That morning, I woke up with a start, because someone had very suddenly opened the curtains around my bed and the bright morning sunlight nearly blinded me even through my closed eyelids. Sitting up, I opened my eyes and saw Carolyn standing at the foot of the bed, wearing her usual scowl.

"Finally, the royal guest awakens," she said with more venom than could possibly be inserted into the sentence.

Before I had the chance to hide behind a calm façade, I let an annoyed "Good morning to you too" escape from my mouth.

Satisfied that she had finally managed to rattle me, she smirked and continued, "The king and queen await you in the Council Chamber. Please dress appropriately, not in the rags you had worn when they brought you here. I will wait in the sitting room and escort you downstairs.

"Alright. Thank you," I replied simply.

Quickly going to brush my teeth and doing the other necessary things to prepare myself for the day, I was back in my room within twenty minutes or so. Luckily,

I had picked out a dress the day before. It was blue – the colour of the summer sky on a cloudless day – with long, flowing sleeves. Although it had a full skirt, I was fairly certain that this was a daytime dress. I also found a blue ribbon and tied back my hair, unsure about women's fashions in Kaleidos. Saying goodbye to Arch and walking out into the sitting room, I could see that Carolyn approved of my appearance even if she would not admit it.

Without a word, she opened the door and led me to the service stairs once again. Clearly, these people did not want me to see their palace. When we reached a level of the castle where I knew the kitchens were directly below, Carolyn opened a door and led me into another dark hallway with shining floors and candles in sconces along the walls. Finally stopping at a heavily guarded door, she said, "Please let His Highness know that the guest has arrived."

One of the guards nodded and went into what I assumed to be the Council Chamber. A minute or two later, he came back out, nodded at Carolyn, and opened the door wide so that I could see into the large room within.

"Aunt Margaret?!" I exclaimed, receiving the worst shock of all since the beginning of this strange adventure.

There she was, the woman I had known for most of my life yet clearly did not know at all. Her black hair was elaborately arranged on top of her head, and she wore a dress in a dark burgundy colour.

"Hello Silvana. Please come in and sit down," she said with a flourish of her manicured hand.

"Yes, Silvana, please sit. We have been expecting you," said a voice to her left, and I looked once again into the black eyes of Julian Cromwell. Today he was dressed in kingly clothing, complete with a velvet cloak that matched Margaret's dress in colour.

Still trying to shake off my disbelief, I nevertheless sat down at the round table across from them, as per their request. "What is going on here?" I asked.

"Would you like the short or long version?" said the king in a mocking tone.

Refusing to dignify him with an answer, I said, "Aunt Margaret, please explain. I received your letter, and aside from everything else, you said that you wanted to protect me from *him*. I assume you were referring to your king, here?"

Showing emotion for the first time, she laughed. "My sweet, naïve girl, did you really believe all that? When your cowardly father ran away from my husband's power into the mortal world, I followed you. Oh yes, we knew you had been born with a rare gift, and we could not allow you to live. Yet your stubborn parents placed various protective spells on you from the day you entered that world – that was the only magic they have ever used since, but it certainly hindered my plans. I knew that the only way to destroy you was to lure you into Kaleidos, where the protective spells were no longer valid, and I had been sure of my success when you discovered the portal. I convinced your parents that I was on their side by buying a piano especially for you and having it installed in my attic, but of course, James and Annabelle were not as naïve as I had hoped – they extended the range of their protective spells, which locked the portal every time you came near it, and I had almost given up. I was even prepared to let your powers simply expire on the day of your 26th birthday, which is only four months away, I believe. Then, you would never again be a danger to us."

Digesting all this new information, I asked, "How was I ever a danger to you in the first place?"

Cromwell had apparently decided to take over the telling of the story, for he answered me: "Weather control, as insignifi-insignificant as it sounds, is our most powerful weapon in this world. That is the purpose of our strong alliance with the Tenebris people, whom my wife comes from. No Cromwell had ever been born with that gift, until you. How do I say this in a way you would understand? You would have totally messed up our political system."

Margaret looked at him with astonishment, while I said, "I can understand proper English, thank you very much. So, how do *you* fit into all of this?"

"When I saw that my wife was failing in her mission, I had no choice but to go into the mortal world myself. Margaret had explained to me that you were at an age when young adults begin searching for employment, and your parents had conveniently destroyed your life's goals. It was only a matter of time until I was able to curse the previous owner of that school bus company and begin looking for you. Unfortunately, your father's protective spells repelled me much more than Margaret --"

"Then how did you find me?"

Margaret replied, "Did never wonder why your hair grows back so quickly after being cut, and every time you try to dye it brown the dye washes off immediately? James' protective spells apparently repel not only Dark Magic but also regular tracking spells, so using a beauty spell was my only option to help King Julian detect you in the mortal world when your magic had almost reached its expiration date. The added benefit was the discomfort you've likely been feeling due to the attention your hair colour receives in your world."

"Yes, thank you very much for that," I said acidly.

The king and queen abruptly rose from their seats, saying, "Now that you know everything, this interview is over."

Too astonished by the story and hurt by the lies and betrayal, I left the Council Chamber without a backward glance and silently followed Carolyn back upstairs.

Memories

Alone in my rooms, I began to pace, deep in contemplation of everything I had just heard. Aunt Margaret was not only spying on my family, she was constantly looking for a way to lure me back here so that her husband could destroy the best chance Kaleidos had of survival. When she realized that my parents used their magic to lock the portal every time I was alone with her and placed a protective spell on me, she dedicated her life to finding another way to destroy me. She had even cursed my hair! Placing a spell on someone so that a powerful possessor of magic – passing himself off as the owner of a school bus company – can trace them is the most random thing I have ever heard. I also had to admit that it was genius.

No longer able to be alone with my thoughts yet having no one here I could talk to, I decided to walk in the palace gardens. Taking a grey cape out of my closet and securing it around my shoulders with a ribbon attached to the hood, I walked quietly down the service stairs to the kitchens. I knew that I was risking another unpleasant encounter with Carolyn, but I would rather see her than any of the royal family.

As I arrived in the kitchens and began to quickly walk to the door, no one spoke to me and no one tried to stop me, and I was so relieved that I did not wonder at the strangeness of this. Walking out into the courtyard at last, I followed a path away from the stables, which I now knew were on the eastern side of the castle, and eventually I reached the gardens. Being too upset to give them more than a brief glance, I forged a path through the apple trees, still replaying my conversation with Margaret in my mind. Though I was still reeling from the betrayal, I couldn't help but think about her claims that I had magical powers. This led me to remember a certain incident that happened back in the third grade...

Skylar and I were friends for a short time with a boy who had a very unfortunate name: Leslie. Although he had clearly asked all of the teachers to call him Les and one of his parents always waited for him in the car after school, one day he forgot his lunch and his mother came to the school to give it to him. When she could not immediately locate him in the crowded cafeteria, she yelled at the top of her lungs,

"Leslie Finch! Where are you? I brought your lunchbox!"

Needless to say, there was no end to the teasing from that moment onwards. While the other children only made half-hearted attempts to mock Les, a group of older, popular boys simply would not leave him alone. No matter what Skylar and I said to them, no matter how many times they were reprimanded by teachers and their own parents, the teasing only became worse as time went by. The boys were in the sixth grade and so they thought they owned the school and everyone in it. Every girl had a crush on the leader, Oliver Montgomery. With dark blond hair and piercing green eyes, he was not only aware of all the attention but rejoiced in it.

Unlike many of the other girls at school, I was not one to fall for a hand-some face alone. Oliver was not a nice boy, and even though I was only eight years old, I did not approve of the fact that he was worshipped by the entire school and clear-ly spoiled by his parents. These same parents were otherwise surprisingly nice people. Being our next-door neighbours, they graciously welcomed us to the neigh-bourhood when we moved back from Sweden and helped my parents get our home furnished and organized. Mr. and

Mrs. Montgomery were also veterinarians, so they immediately formed a bond with my parents over their interest in the general medical field. They tried to forge a friendship between me and Oliver, but he always hid in his room when my family was invited to their home.

One day, Skylar and I were playing hide-and-seek with a few other girls at recess while Les played tetherball with some of his friends. From my hiding place inside a plastic house set aside for the kindergarteners, I kept one eye on the tetherball game, especially when Oliver and his gang decided to join in. I was immediately worried about my friend, but all I could do was watch the events unfold because Les was adamant that he will not be known as someone who needs a girl to protect him. Aside from a few mean yet harmless comments shouted by the older boys, however, everything was going smoothly. Then Oliver caught the ball and hurled it with all his strength at the unsuspecting Les, hitting him in the chest and making him fall to the ground.

I was standing between bully and victim before I realized that I had moved. "Leave. Him. Alone," I said to Oliver, enunciating each word.

Oliver and his gang just laughed. "Why should I? Because little Leslie will tell her mummy?" he asked.

I pretended to think and then said, "Maybe I will tell your mum."

Clearly, that was a mistake, for Oliver's gang howled with laughter once more while he said, "Go ahead."

He then began to turn away, but I yanked on his arm to turn him back to face me. That was when he pushed me. I fell to the ground, almost hitting my head on the pole to which the tetherball was attached. Blinking tears from my eyes, I noticed that by then Les had stood up and the rest of the school began to gather around the scene. I briefly wondered where all the teachers were, but I was so angry that all I wanted to do was avenge myself, Les, and everyone else who ever fell victim to Oliver's cruelty. All of a sudden, the previously cloudless sky was engulfed by dark clouds and a heavy rain had started. Then, a lightning bolt had come out of nowhere and struck the ground between Oliver and myself. The rest of the school began to run, screaming, back indoors, urged by teachers who belatedly began to appear. I felt, more than saw or heard, Skylar help me up from the ground. My gaze was locked with Oliver's, who stood looking at me with horror in his eyes. Later, Skylar told me that my own eyes had turned dark blue – the colour of a stormy sea – and my entire body seemed to glow with a faint blue light. She asked if I had magical powers, but I just laughed at her and we soon forgot the entire incident.

Oliver, however, looked at me with a new respect from that day on. A few days later, which also happened to be Valentine's Day, he suddenly sat down with Skylar and me at lunch and gave me a chocolate bar. He also apologized to Les and made sure that no one ever teased him again. When our parents spent time together, he always came downstairs to entertain me while they talked.

He soon began throwing rocks at my window so that I would meet him outside, and he took me to the park where he purposely sought out stray or injured animals and brought them to his parents for the necessary care. By then, he was about to move on to high school and I was just graduating from elementary school. That summer, we started a dog-walking business in our neighbourhood, which quickly turned into pet-sitting for those who needed it. He also revealed his dream to one day work in an animal sanctuary, and I fully supported him in that. He, meanwhile, loved listening to me play the piano and I soon began to develop my skills by writing songs inspired by our friendship.

My relationship with Oliver almost rivaled my friendship with Skylar, and yet as we got older and girls began to take a romantic interest in him, he began to drift away from me. When I was fifteen, Oliver was eighteen and on his way to the University of Zurich for a double-major in Evolutionary Biology and Environmental Studies. He promised to stay until my sixteenth birthday on August 12, but a week before the big event he said that his girlfriend – who always seemed threatened by me for no reason whatsoever – wanted to go on a trip with him before they went to separate universities. When I let them know that I was upset, she demanded that he choose between her and me. He chose me. On my birthday, he said that he had always loved me and I realized that I felt the same way...

Not particularly liking the direction my thoughts had taken, I tried to clear my mind by lightly shaking my head.

Trapped

"Are you alright?" asked a vaguely familiar voice behind me.

I turned towards the voice and saw Prince Gideon. Today he was not wearing armour but a medieval outfit, complete with something resembling a vest over a long-sleeved tunic. The colour scheme of his clothing was the white, black and yellow of the Cromwell crest, which strangely suited him. It also took the attention away from his terrifying black eyes.

Sinking into a curtsey that felt strangely natural despite the long skirts I was wearing, I said, "I'm fine. Good afternoon, Your Highness."

"Please, call me Gideon," he said, reminding me of my very first conversation with Esmeralda. He stood up from the bench he had been sitting on and asked, "What were you thinking of just then? You looked troubled."

Somewhat touched by his concern but not quite trusting him, I replied, "It's nothing. I simply miss my home and someone very special to me. We parted recently. It was my choice, but now I might be starting to regret it."

"Even so, if he let you go, he never deserved you in the first place," said the prince with surprising conviction.

"I appreciate your saying that, but you don't even know me," I replied.

Offering me his arm, he asked, "Shall we take a walk? I will explain everything."

I took his arm, which seemed to be the polite response, and we began a slow walk among the trees. Yet a minute or two later, his previous statement reminded me that these were the exact words he had said to me when he left me in the courtyard the previous night. My distrust came back full force, but I managed to regain my composure and attempt to find out his involvement in his parents' schemes.

"Gideon, I have a question," I began carefully. "Last night you said that 'we' will explain everything, yet you did not attend the meeting I had with your parents this morning. How much do you know of what we discussed?"

Laughing, he said, "I know everything. You are a regular girl who somehow activated the magical portal we use to travel between Kaleidos and the mortal world. I would assume my father explained the existence of this parallel universe, but that is all there is to it."

So he doesn't even know that I may very well be his cousin and the daughter of the previous king, I thought to myself. Aloud, I said, "But how do you explain that you know that I know about your father's frequent visits to my world?"

"Did you not once catch him disappearing into the portal and eventually decide to investigate?"

I stopped and, despite my fear, looked into his eyes. Like his voice, his eyes seemed sincere and he did not break eye-contact as I expect a liar would have done. Bracing myself for what I knew I had to do in order to perhaps gain an ally, I began, "Gideon, there's something I need to tell you."

Still with the same sincerity on his face, he said, "Yes?"

Suddenly, I felt something heavy land on my head and I lost consciousness.

I woke up in my own bed, quite soon after the incident, judging by the position of the sun in the afternoon sky. I touched the back of my head, and miraculously found no sign of the injury I had suffered. Carefully standing and finding that I was steady on my feet, I ran to my front door and touched the handle. It was locked!

"Help!! I'm locked in here!" I yelled, banging on the door with all my strength. "Please, someone help me!"

After several minutes, I heard footsteps in the hallway, followed by someone inserting a key into the lock on my door. Stepping back yet preparing to run out, I was surprised to find that it was only Esmeralda. She came inside, balancing a tray on one hand, and promptly closed the door behind her.

"Esmeralda? What is going on?" I asked her.

"I'm so sorry, but this is how it must be," she replied, not making any sense whatsoever.

"What are you talking about?"

"The truth is, Carolyn overheard you telling the prince something you should have kept secret, and she had no choice but to have me climb a tree and drop a heavy apple on your head. It had to be inconspicuous."

"You do realize that you are not making any sense, right? Why were you both in the gardens? And did the prince not say anything when -- whatever this was, happened to me?"

Clearly uncomfortable with my interrogation, Esmeralda said evasively, "We said it was an accident."

Placing the tray on the table in the sitting room, she began backing away towards the door, saying, "Now, I'm truly sorry, but I must lock you in here again. Believe me – it is for your own good."

Before I had the chance to react, or better yet, stop her, she slid out of a small opening in the doorway and swiftly slammed the door shut after her. By the time I ran to the door and tried to push it open, she had already locked it and I heard her hurried footsteps retreating. I wished that Arch wasn't the kind of dog who easily takes a liking to people. If he had tried to attack Esmeralda in that "poodle way" of his, I might have had an extra ten seconds to stop her from locking me in again. Instead, he was asleep in his basket and only gave a half-hearted bark when my captor entered the room.

Knowing that I was no longer welcome – that perhaps I never had been – I began planning my escape. My only option was the window, and I was not looking forward to climbing down the sheer face of the castle, yet I had no other choice. I changed back into my jeans and boots, put on my jacket, and tied Arch onto my back with one of the extra blankets. Then, I opened the window and looked down, preparing for my descent.

For the first time feeling lucky that Oliver had taken me rock-climbing several times in the years that I've known him, I carefully stepped out onto the window ledge and began my precarious climb down the castle wall. Luckily, no windows were in my direct path, and I managed to avoid the ones that were close. Arch must have sensed the danger, for he did not move and thus remained secure in the makeshift carrier on my back. When I finally reached the courtyard, I found all the guards sleeping at their posts. *What a nice security system they have here*, I thought to myself, as I quietly stepped around them and walked out of the open gates. In hindsight, I realized that I should thank the universe for the cover of darkness – the events in my room and the climb must have taken longer than I thought

Trudging through the snow on foot was much more difficult than on horseback, but I knew that I could not give up. My will to escape this terrible place was so strong that it drove me onwards, despite the cold, despite the hunger, and despite the knowledge that I could be missed and followed at any moment. When I finally reached the woods, I checked my still-working watch and found that I had only been walking for two hours, and that gave me additional courage to find the clearing where the mirror portal had been. I was surprised to find that it was very close to the edge of the woods. *Had Cromwell been trying to confuse me, when he led me around in circles yesterday?*

Now came the most difficult part of all: Summoning the mirror. I tried waving my arms and willing the mirror to appear with my mind, I even tried to summon rain or lightning the way I had done at least once before, all to no avail.

Frustrated, I said, "Open Sesame?" But, of course, that did not work either.

Esmeralda's Story

I stopped my unsuccessful attempts to summon the mirror when I heard Arch softly growling from within the blanket. Only then did I realize that, determined as I was to return home and get away from this strange place, I was alone in the woods quite late in the evening. Had the ground not been covered with snow, I might have had a chance to climb a tree before any animal or human could attack me. In the current weather conditions, however, something or someone would have the advantage of muffled footsteps if I, the potential victim, was not paying attention. At least I had thought of picking up a sturdy stick I could use as a weapon. And yet, I had not only myself but also my dog to protect, so I quickly whispered: "Arch, shhhh! We might be in danger."

"Don't worry, Silvana, it's just me," said a voice, and to my relief Esmeralda walked out of the darkness in the trees directly in front of where I was standing.

I was still slightly wary of her, considering that she stood by and allowed Carolyn to treat me the way she did, so I asked, "And why exactly would I not worry? Have you finally decided to join my side and help me?"

Instead of answering, she suddenly collapsed at my feet, sobbing. I knelt down and tried to put my arm around her shoulders, but she shook me off. "You don't understand – she forced me to do this to you! I wanted to tell you the truth from the start, but she threatened to throw me out, and then how would I survive?"

"Who, Carolyn? Doesn't your world have any human rights laws?" I asked, confused.

"Human rights laws? What are those?" she asked, equally confused.

"I'll tell you later. Please go on," I said, smiling. I could now see that we had a common enemy because no one, not even the most talented actress, could cry in such a heart-rending way.

Hesitating only slightly, she replied, "I think it's time that you heard the truth about your family, and some of the untold history of this place. Please do not be angry with me. I was only an innocent victim of my mother's schemes."

"Who is your mother?"

"Carolyn."

I digested this information surprisingly well. Subconsciously, I knew from the very beginning that these two women, as different as they were in personality, had a very distinct similarity in looks. Instead of replying, I stood and offered my hand to Esmeralda to help her stand. When she looked at me with evident confusion, I explained, "It looks like we have a long talk ahead of us, and I'd rather not continue sitting in the snow. I saw a log in another clearing not too far from here. Let us go sit there."

She stood up without my help, nodding in agreement.

I picked up my dog, saying "Sorry Arch, it looks like we won't be going home just yet," and the three of us relocated to the log about a ten-minute walk away.

We sat down, adjusted our respective cloaks around ourselves to keep warm in the dark winter forest, and Esmeralda began her story:

"Thirty years ago, your father was crowned king of Kaleidos and the land was prosperous and happy. Your grandfather had created incredibly close alliances with the nearby counties, and they were glad to share all the powers at their disposal to help us protect our world.

The county of Tenebris, however, once threatened to destroy our world with their ability to control the weather unless your grandfather allowed their leader's daughter to marry into the royal family. James was already betrothed to Annabelle, so your grandfather offered his younger son Julian instead. The Tenebris people accepted and everyone thought the threat was permanently gone.

What none of them knew was that Julian had a secret relationship with one of the maids, and I think he truly loved her. He promised to marry her regardless of what his family thought, so he was furious when he found out about his forced betrothal to the Tenebris girl. Meanwhile, James knew about the secret relationship and tried to help his brother. He convinced Julian to obey your grandfather's wishes, while the maid would be promoted to Head of the Household and would be well taken care of. She, however, was very unhappy about this turn of events, so she ran away from the castle one night and disappeared for a while.

One year later, she came back very suddenly and asked King James for her old job back. Your father was still mourning the premature death of your grandfather, so he could not bring himself to once again hurt the young woman. He not only took her back but also gave her the Head of the Household position. She was extremely grateful, and eventually she even stopped avoiding Julian and his new wife.

Meanwhile, Julian was unhappy at not being crowned king, and he made a secret agreement with his wife's people to teach him to control the weather. He also obtained forbidden books on Dark Magic, and when his weather magic turned fully Dark, he began planning to overthrow his brother and take Kaleidos for himself.

Three years later, the king's daughter was born with the very rare gift of controlling the weather, but her magic was different – it was more powerful and could eventually be used for good instead of evil as her powers developed. She could be Kaleidos' greatest protector, and yet her powers also endangered her life. Fearing his brother's magic, James went into hiding in the mortal world with his wife and daughter, choosing his family over his kingdom. Forsaking the name of James Cromwell, King and High Protector of Kaleidos, he became James Doyle – a regular British dentist.

With the king gone, the Head of the Household finally thought it was safe to bring her three-year-old daughter to the palace. There was no question who her father was, yet Julian refused to acknowledge the girl's existence and the girl's mother's anger began to grow once again. One day during Julian's weekly meeting to discuss political affairs, she burst into the council room and began accusing Julian of everything except his true crime. He became so angry that he called upon the Tenebris powers and caused an eternal winter in our world, so that no one would ever dare to question his authority again. Rumours were that this is what turned his blood cold and made his eyes black and lifeless.

That brings us to this day. As you might have guessed, Carolyn was Julian's first love and I am their daughter. An unknown power has held my mother prisoner, not allowing her to quit her job, which resulted in my being appointed as one of the maids in her charge. The story was forgotten by everyone except those involved, and my mother and I were able to finally put it behind us. That is, until she saw you and it brought back memories of her anger towards your father for not doing more to protect her relationship with Julian, and that is why she hates you. I am so sorry."

While Esmeralda was telling her story, she did not look at me, but now she turned to see my reaction.

I interrupted my own shocked silence with just one statement: "So that means Julian is my uncle and Carolyn is my aunt. You are my cousin. And so is Gideon, just as I suspected."

"Yes," she replied quietly.

"Margaret told me that she followed us into the mortal world to get rid of me. Is that why my parents left England for Sweden?"

"Yes, I think so."

"I cannot believe she eventually convinced them that she was on our side!"

"Do not blame them, Silvana. They were probably tired of the secrets and the constant hiding, like my mother and I," Esmeralda said.

I simply nodded. I now knew what I needed to do to save Kaleidos from the tyranny of Julian Cromwell. I did not get the chance to share my plan with my long-lost cousin, however, because a bolt of lightning suddenly struck the log close to where she was sitting. It came not from the sky but from the darkness on our right.

Ambushed

Screaming in fright, Esmeralda jumped off the log and tried to run, but another of light – blue and emitting icy air that I could feel even on this cold night – came out of the darkness and struck her back. She gave a cry of pain and stopped mid-step, quickly turning blue from head to toe. In my state of shock, I could see every horrible detail in slow motion, and because of that I understood with painful clarity that she was frozen. And there was only one person who could have done that to her.

Finally standing up from the log, I turned towards the man who rode out of the dark trees on his white horse. He was dressed in armour once again, and the visor of his helmet was raised above his face, making his black eyes all the more terrifying. Although I was well aware of the guards he had brought with him – or the "silent army," as I had initially thought of them – all I could think of was avenging my cousin, my family, and Kaleidos itself. Before Cromwell could utter a word, I gathered all my negative emotions, and as my hands began to glow with a blue light I flung my new-found power at him. All I managed to create, however, was a dark cloud above his head and a rain shower that was barely beyond a drizzle. As Julian moved his horse out from under the cloud, he and his entire guard began to laugh.

"This is what I was afraid of? The legendary High Protector of Kaleidos whose powers are only fit for watering flowers?" he asked with scorn.

Knowing that his questions were rhetorical, I replied nonetheless, "At least my powers are real. I did not have to lie and cheat the Tenebris out of their secrets. If I had had a fair chance, I have no doubt that I would have defeated you."

"Oh, but you have only your father to blame for that, my dear," he said, feigning sympathy. "He was always weak, and now I see that so are you."

"If he was so weak, why did you go to all this trouble to try to overthrow him? Why not simply challenge him to a duel while he was still here?" I asked with equal scorn.

It was clear that I had hit my mark because he did not reply, yet his eyes betrayed his rage with a hint of shame. His guards, meanwhile, had drawn their swords in their silent way and began surrounding me. I knew that I could not win this fight, and I was mentally preparing to die. Then I thought of one more thing: *Where is Arch?* He did not make a sound when he should have sensed Cromwell's approach. I looked at the ground near the log and froze in shock. My dog had been turned into an ice sculpture, probably while Esmeralda and I were talking.

My eyes filled with tears despite my attempts to maintain my calm façade, and I knelt on the ground beside him. "No..." I said.

I heard Cromwell's cruel laughter once more, and as I looked up I saw him raise his hand to freeze me as well.

"Stop!" yelled a male voice on the other side of the clearing. "Stop this madness!"

As I looked towards the voice, I was surprised to find several men and women walking out from among the dark trees. There was nothing distinctive about these people, except for their fully black clothing and the fact that they were barefoot. Yet they did not look cold – they seemed to emit warmth that spread all around them and even reached me. Their leader was an elderly man who carried a staff that was crowned with a yellow jewel, emitting more of the magical warmth.

Cromwell quickly lowered his hand and said in a respectful tone, "Good evening, Orlando."

"Is it truly a good evening, my king? We were on our way back from gathering moonlight when we saw two young women being ambushed by an entire army for no reason that I can fathom," the elderly man replied.

"They were breaking our most sacred law – telling lies about the royal family. The punishment for treason is death!"

"My king, I have always respected your father and then your brother, but you? You are no longer the brave young man to whom I gave my daughter in marriage. I believe every word the young ladies were saying, and I have just witnessed your niece show great, although evidently untrained, power. We cannot allow you to rule this way any longer!" said the leader of the Tenebris, as he obviously was.

He raised his staff and his companions simultaneously raised their hands, but before they could do any more than this Cromwell did the most horrifying thing I had seen yet: With one wave of his hand, he had conjured the mirror, but instead of opening the portal he set off a bolt of his icy, blue light that glanced off the mirror's surface and expanded to several times its size. The light hit the Tenebris people and instantly froze them.

With a satisfied, evil smirk, Cromwell turned to me and said, "Now who is weak? I wish you the best of luck with this, my dear niece."

Then, he turned his horse and followed his already retreating guards, out of the clearing and in the direction of the palace.

Justice at Last

I've always believed that sometimes you have to lose a small battle in order to win the big war. We might have been ambushed and overpowered, but I've been given a secret weapon that could destroy the so-called king and bring peace to Kaleidos at last.

Instead of crying in self-pity, I decided that my first step was figuring out a way to unfreeze the Tenebris people as well as Esmeralda and Arch. I thought of all the fairytales I've seen and read, both old and new, and found the one theme they all have in common: Love conquers all. I picked up my frozen dog and hugged him, ignoring the discomfort of touching solid ice, not to mention the emotional pain of seeing him this way. I hugged him and sent all the positive emotions I had left into his frozen body. A few slow, agonizing minutes later, I felt him stir and press his wet nose against my cheek. My plan had worked!

Placing Arch on the ground, where he promptly began running around and sniffing at the frozen humans' feet, I walked over to where Esmeralda stood and hugged her, thinking of the great risk she took in following me all the way from the castle and into the woods, and telling me her secret. When I saw colour returning to her face, I stepped away, and soon she spoke: "Silvana? You saved me!"

"I guess I did!" I replied, smiling for the first time in what felt like forever. "Now, we don't have much time. I need to figure out a way to unfreeze the Tenebris without having to hug each of them."

"The Tenebris? They are on Cromwell's side!" Esmeralda warned me.

I quickly explained to her what happened after she was attacked, and she sighed in relief. "It looks like we have someone on our side after all." She paused. "Silvana? Have you tried gathering all your positive emotions and sending them into the air above?"

Intuition told me that she was right, and I smiled once more. Closing my eyes, I thought of all the wonderful people I had in my life. My parents, who abandoned their kingdom to protect their only daughter. Skylar, who was there for me through all the ups and downs of growing up and all the smiles and tears of early adulthood. Oliver, who was also there for me through everything, and even though I had hurt him simply because of his success and my failure at life, I knew that he would never try to hurt me back. And then there was my new friend Esmeralda and my wonderful dog. These thoughts made me feel like I haven't felt in a long time: happy and light. I also felt warm, and I knew that I was probably glowing with the blue light. I raised my hands into the air and felt the power, much stronger than when I tried to attack the king, leave my fingertips and spread all around me.

I stood this way for several minutes, and when I finally opened my eyes, I saw the unfrozen group of Tenebris looking at me with a mix of shock and awe. I was shocked as well when I looked down and found us all standing on dark grass.

Seeing me notice them, the Tenebris kneeled as one, and the leader said, "My lady, you are the true queen of Kaleidos and we are forever in your debt."

I walked towards the elderly man and lightly touched his shoulder. "Please stand up," I said. "I am honoured to have discovered this power, but the war is far from over."

As he stood, followed by the other Tenebris, Orlando said, "We are behind you, my queen, but we might not have to engage in battle. The people of Kaleidos have feared Julian for so long that they have lost any respect they ever had for him. I can guarantee that they will believe you when you tell them the truth. And we will be there to verify every word!" he vowed. "Also, his son has no idea about any of this. He may be an asset to us."

"In that case, is there a way to reach the castle quickly from here?" I asked with equal parts determination and eagerness.

The kindly elder smiled. "Close your eyes and call upon your power, but instead of channeling it into your hands, think of where you'd like to go and you will be transported there. We will meet you there soon."

"Thank you very much! I will never forget this," I said to him, then offered my hand to Esmeralda. "Will you come with me?"

She nodded, picked up my dog, and took my hand. Closing my eyes, I did just as Orlando instructed.

When I opened my eyes, Esmeralda and I were standing not only in Cromwell Castle but in the wing where the prince's rooms were located. Letting go of my cousin's reassuring hand, I marched with purpose towards the prince's rooms. I did not care that it was the middle of the night and that I would not be allowed to see him for precisely that reason – all I cared about was restoring order and administering justice where it was due, once and for all. When I reached the door, I spoke before the guards could stop me: "I demand to see Prince Gideon immediately!"

Nearly betraying his astonishment, one of the guards replied, "I'm afraid I cannot allow it, Miss Doyle. The prince is asleep."

"Please, this can't wait! The entire fate of the kingdom depends on what we have to tell him!"

As the guards continued to protest, I heard footsteps approaching and turned around. Someone must have woken Carolyn, for she was walking towards us while hastily tying an apron over her nightgown.

"Miss Doyle! This is highly inappropriate!" she tried to admonish me.

"I'll tell you what is truly inappropriate, Aunt Carolyn: Lying to the entire kingdom!" I said.

Turning to Esmeralda, Carolyn exclaimed, "You told her!"

"Yes, *Mother*," replied her daughter. "I couldn't live like this anymore."

Before Carolyn could react, the door opened and out walked Gideon himself. "What is all this commotion?" he asked.

I took and deep breath, preparing myself to repeat everything I had heard from
both Margaret and Esmeralda. Normally I
would never stoop to blackmail – it goes
against my morals and everything I believe
in – but after all the things Julian had
done, all the lives he had destroyed, I knew
that his son needed to know the truth.

After that, everything unfolded very
quickly. Gideon believed me without question, and he immediately sent several
guards to wake and arrest his father for
treason. He also arranged for Carolyn and
Esmeralda to take over two of the best
rooms in the palace, and he threatened to
arrest his mother as well if she did not
treat them as equals from that moment
onwards. When the Tenebris people finally
arrived at the palace, Gideon welcomed
them with open arms and thanked them
for saving his sisters from Julian's wrath.
Orlando was named Chief Advisor to the
Prince – soon to be Chief Advisor to the
Queen, when I were to return.

While I tried to help Gideon restore order to the kingdom, he said that I was
needed elsewhere: at home in my own
world. Promising to give me credit for end-
ing the eternal winter and to arrange my
coronation as soon as I came back to Kaleidos, he said that will happily step aside.

I was touched by the gesture and made my own promise, to leave him in charge for the time being.

Bidding farewell to my newly discovered cousins, I went to my royal rooms to clean myself up after the long and eventful night. Then, I picked up my dog and transported us back to the clearing where I had first stepped out of the mirror.

By this time, it was morning and the forest presented itself to me in all its spring glory. The trees surrounding me were covered in emerald-coloured leaves, the wildflowers in the clearing were in full bloom, and birds flew overhead, singing their happy melodies. I looked up to see the still snow-capped mountains standing out beautifully against the background of the brilliant blue sky. The world had shaken off winter's slumber and was bursting with life once again.

Smiling, I summoned the mirror, which was no trouble at all this time, and watched as the portal opened up before my eyes.

Epilogue

As I stepped over the threshold into my own world, I knew that I would be coming back to Kaleidos. I might have defeated Julian with something as simple as truth and logic, but I was not quite sure that I could trust his current state of imprisonment – he had magical powers, after all. Luckily, Gideon was on my side. Considering that his father lied to him his entire life, it was quite plausible that he would protect the kingdom for someone who finally told him the truth. And who knows, maybe we could truly be friends one day. I just hoped that Esmeralda would forgive her mother. It's true that Carolyn's bitterness is very well justified, but placing the burden of such a secret on her daughter was cruel. I can certainly understand why my cousin was so eager to confide in someone who was finally on her side. In fact, she promised to visit me in London one day – I hoped that she would.

So, I had completely forgotten that I had been gone for two days, and I highly doubted that this strange fairytale I had just experienced went as far as having time flow differently in Kaleidos so that no one would have noticed my absence. As I walked through the mirror into my aunt's attic room, I was somewhat surprised to hear sirens outside the house. I was even more surprised to see Skylar sitting at the piano in tears, holding the bag I had left behind. When she saw me, the grief on her face turned to a mix of relief and shock, and before I knew it she had grabbed me into a bone-crushing hug.

"Oh my god! Where have you been! How could you do this to me! I hate you right now!" she exclaimed, still crying and hugging me.

I laughed and stepped back to look at my best friend. "Make up your mind! Are you happy to see me or are you mad?" I asked.

"Both!" she replied, laughing in spite of herself.

"I hate to interrupt this sister reunion, but there's someone here who had missed you as well," said a voice I never thought I would hear again.

I looked up into the eyes of Oliver, and we exchanged a look more meaningful than words could ever be. My eyes expressed the deepest regret and apology for hurting him for no reason, and his eyes expressed nothing but love and understanding.

Before I could say anything, however, Skylar said, "We kind of need to go cancel the missing person's report I filed, and then you have a lot of explaining to do, young lady!"

"I know, although I doubt that you will believe me," I replied.

Oliver finally stepped forward and put his arm around my shoulders. "Don't worry, Silvana, I trust you no matter what."

"I know you do," I said with a smile.

With that, the three of us headed downstairs. I was mentally preparing myself to explain to the police my emotional breakdown that led me to leave my bag with my phone, as well as all my money and identification, and stay with my cousin for over two days without telling anyone. That wasn't technically a lie, just a story with a few details omitted. Skylar and Oliver would hear the truth, of course, and if they didn't believe me I was fairly sure that I could prove it. Especially after talking to my parents, who had a lot of explaining to do as well. For one thing, I wanted to know why my mother had given up her piano and only allowed me to pursue my own talents while it was nothing more than a hobby. I was sincerely hoping that we would reconcile and become a close family once more. After all, I am Silvana Cromwell, Queen and High Protector of Kaleidos – I would likely become Silvana Montgomery someday soon, but that is another story for another time – and nothing would keep me from fulfilling my duties yet being happy in both worlds ever again.

Glossary

Kaleidos: Taken from the word "kaleido-scope," which is derived from the Ancient Greek *kalos* (beautiful), *eidos* (shape), and *skopeō* (to examine). Essentially, "the observation of beautiful shapes." This word was chosen as the name of the parallel universe to which Silvana travels simply for the way that it sounds.

Tenebris: The Latin word for "darkness." This word was also chosen simply for the way that it sounds, as the name of Kaleidos' closest ally.

About the Author

Diana Spektor began writing as soon as she learned how to read, composing fantastical tales and keeping a diary. In later youth and early adulthood, she also began writing poetry. She is often inspired by her favourite authors: William Shakespeare, Jane Austen, and J.R.R. Tolkien. Her first published literary work is *From the Heart: Reflections on Life*, a collection of poetry. *Beyond the Mirror* is her debut novel.

Ms. Spektor is also an avid reader and aspiring editor. She currently resides in Toronto, Ontario, with her hamster Sophie and other undisclosed family members.